Three Hundred Miles to Tehran

By

Grady Lee Honeycutt

"This book would not have been possible without the
encouragement of Kaelyn Owens."

Table of Contents

Prologue

Some journeys begin with careful planning. Others begin quietly, without warning, long before anyone realizes the path ahead will lead into history.

In the late 1970s, Iran stood at the center of a rapidly shifting world. On the surface, the country appeared stable and prosperous under the rule of the Shah. Oil money flowed, modernization projects expanded across the landscape, and foreign companies worked alongside Iranian officials to build industries, infrastructure, and agricultural systems meant to transform the nation. To outsiders, it looked like progress moving forward at full speed.

Beneath that progress, however, something else was growing.

Across towns and cities, conversations were changing. Workers whispered about politics. Religious leaders spoke more boldly. Demonstrations appeared in places where silence had once been expected. What began as scattered unrest slowly grew into something much larger—an undercurrent of anger and frustration that few outsiders fully understood at the time.

For the many Americans living and working in Iran during those years, life often continued in a strange balance between normal routine and quiet uncertainty. Engineers, technicians, contractors, and advisors arrived from the United States to support projects tied to agriculture, aviation, energy, and military modernization. They traveled the country, lived among local communities, and carried out the work they had been hired to do.

Most believed they were witnessing a country moving forward.

Very few realized they were standing on the edge of a revolution.

History tends to focus on leaders, governments, and major events, but the truth is that history is also lived by ordinary people who simply happen to be present when the world shifts. Sometimes they arrive by chance. Sometimes they follow an opportunity that seems straightforward at the time. Only later do they understand that they had stepped into something far bigger than the job they originally accepted.

This story is about one of those journeys.

It is a story about a man who found himself working inside a country that was quietly moving toward upheaval. A story about travel through unfamiliar landscapes, encounters with cultures far different from home, and the strange situations that arise when politics, business, and everyday life collide.

More than anything, it is a story about how quickly the world can change—and what it feels like to be caught in the middle when it does.

Chapter 1

The phone was ringing as I came through the door. I had to pee, but I answered it anyway. It was a Friday afternoon, and I had just gotten home from work. The man on the other end asked me if I was Grady Honeycutt; I answered in the affirmative. He began telling me about a job across the pond, and he thought I might be a good fit for it. He wanted to know if I was interested in talking to him about it. I said yes.

For a moment, I just stood there in the hallway, my briefcase still hanging from my hand and my coat half off my shoulders. The day had been long and ordinary, the kind that blurs together with every other weekday, yet the call instantly made it feel different. I could hear the quiet hum of the refrigerator in the kitchen and the faint sound of traffic passing outside, small reminders that I had just stepped into the routine comfort of home. But the voice on the phone carried the promise of something far from routine.

He spoke calmly and deliberately, as if he had made dozens of these calls before. The way he described the opportunity made it sound both serious and intriguing. It involved travel, responsibility, and work that apparently required someone with my particular background. I listened carefully, trying to piece together exactly how he had come across my name. The idea of a job "across the pond" sounded distant and slightly unreal, like something meant for someone else's life rather than my own.

Still standing there, I shifted the phone to my other ear and leaned against the wall. My mind began racing ahead of the conversation. I pictured unfamiliar streets, foreign accents, and the kind of experiences that only come from leaving everything comfortable behind. At the same time, another part of me wondered whether this was legitimate or simply one of those strange coincidences that sometimes interrupt an otherwise ordinary day.

The man continued explaining that he had been given my name through a professional contact who believed I had the right qualifications.

Apparently, the position required someone adaptable, someone willing to take on challenges that might not always follow a predictable schedule. His tone suggested confidence that I could handle it, though we had never spoken before.

By then, my initial urgency to get to the bathroom had faded, replaced by curiosity. I asked a few questions—where exactly the job was located, how long the assignment might last, and what kind of work it involved. He answered patiently, giving just enough information to keep my interest while hinting that the full details would come later if I was willing to continue the conversation.

Standing there in my quiet house, I realized how strange the moment felt. Only minutes earlier, I had been thinking about nothing more than the end of the workday and the comfort of being home. Now I was listening to a stranger describe an opportunity that could potentially take me halfway across the world.

When he finally paused, he repeated his earlier question, asking again whether I would be interested in discussing the job further. I looked around my empty living room as if expecting someone to offer advice, but of course, there was no one there. Sometimes life presents a choice without warning, and the only thing you can do is decide whether to ignore it or lean toward the unknown.

So I told him yes.

He wanted me to come to his office. His office was about an hour away; I told him I could be there next Friday. He said no. He needed to see me on Monday morning.

Chapter 2

I knew this might be a big opportunity for me, but I didn't have a resume. I did have an old Royal typewriter.

It sat on a small desk in the corner of my living room, a heavy black machine that had already lived through many years before it ever came into my hands. The keys were worn smooth from use, and the ribbon sometimes faded halfway down the page, but it still worked if you treated it with patience. That evening, I pulled a chair up to the desk and rolled a sheet of paper into the carriage, listening to the small mechanical click as it locked into place.

The problem was that I had never needed a resume before. Most of the work I had done came through people who already knew me. Jobs had started with a conversation or a handshake, not a neatly typed document listing experience and qualifications. Now I was staring at a blank sheet of paper, trying to turn the scattered pieces of my work history into something that looked organized and respectable.

I began slowly. I typed my name at the top of the page and paused for a moment, looking at the letters as if they might offer some direction. Then I started listing the jobs I had held, the duties I could remember, and the few skills that seemed worth putting down. Each key struck the paper with a sharp sound that filled the quiet room. Every word felt permanent, since mistakes meant pulling the page out and starting again.

The house was quiet that night except for the steady tapping of the typewriter keys. Outside, the evening had settled in, and the faint glow of the desk lamp reflected in the window beside me. I worked carefully, line by line, trying to keep the page neat. Every so often, I would lean back in the chair and read what I had written, wondering whether it would sound convincing to a man who seemed to have serious expectations.

When I made a mistake, I had to stop, remove the page, and begin again with a fresh sheet of paper. It slowed the process, but it also forced me to think about each line before typing it. Gradually, the page began to fill with a record of where I had been and what I had done.

As the resume took shape, a quiet excitement began to build. Only a few hours earlier, I had been thinking about nothing more than getting home from work. Now I was preparing for a meeting that might send me somewhere far beyond the familiar places in my life.

When I finished the final line, I pulled the paper from the machine and held it under the light. It was not perfect, but it was the best resume I could produce with the tools I had. I placed it carefully on the desk and glanced at the clock.

Monday morning was coming quickly, and whatever waited for me in that office an hour away already felt like the beginning of something new.

On the way to his office, I stopped at a small store and picked up a few file folders to carry the resume in. I chose the neatest one I could find, hoping it would make the whole thing look a little more professional. It felt important that the first impression look organized, even if everything inside the folder had been put together in a rush the night before.

The drive to his office took about an hour, and the entire way I kept thinking about what I might say when I walked through the door. I rehearsed answers to questions he might ask and wondered if my resume would make any kind of impression. By the time I arrived, my nerves were stretched tight.

Chapter 3

When I was escorted into his office, the standard greetings followed. We shook hands and exchanged a few words of polite conversation, but I was immediately intimidated by the man standing in front of me. He was tall and impeccably dressed, the kind of presence that filled a room without effort. When he shook my hand, he looked straight into my eyes. It was the kind of direct, steady look that only comes from someone who already knows where he stands in the world.

I handed him the story of my working life inside the Dollar General folder. He placed it on his desk without opening it. For a moment, I watched the folder sit there between us, thinking about the long night I had spent typing and correcting every line.

A small wave of disappointment passed through me. All those hours of work now rested in front of him, untouched.

Then he looked at me and said, "We know everything about you that we need to know."

He told me the job was in Iran and dismissed any concerns about a language barrier. According to him, everyone there spoke English. The way he said it made the whole situation sound simple, almost routine, as if traveling halfway around the world was no more complicated than crossing a state line.

I was paired with an Iraqi named Fanar, a tall, dark, well-dressed man who worked for the company. He carried himself with quiet confidence and spoke with a calm, measured tone. From the moment we met, it was clear that he already understood how things were supposed to move forward. I felt less like a partner and more like someone being guided along a path that had already been planned.

Chapter 4

On Wednesday, we flew to Washington, D.C., to secure my travel documents. I had never gone through anything like that before, and the entire process felt strangely quick. The only identification I carried with me was my driver's license. I remember thinking that surely they would need more than that, but Fanar did not seem worried.

At the passport office, he disappeared for a while to meet with his contacts. I sat in a waiting area, unsure of exactly what he was arranging behind closed doors. Eventually, someone called my name, took my photograph, and told us to come back in an hour. The whole interaction was brief and almost casual.

With time to spare, Fanar suggested we go to lunch. We walked to a nearby restaurant and sat down like two ordinary travelers passing time between errands. He spoke very little about the details of the trip. Most of the conversation stayed light, almost deliberately ordinary. I sensed that there were things he knew that he was not ready to explain.

After we finished eating, we returned to the office. A short time later, I walked out with a passport in my hand.

It took years for the gravity of that moment to sink in. At the time, I was mostly focused on the excitement of what lay ahead. Only later did the details begin to settle in my mind. I had no birth certificate with me, yet no one ever asked for one. They did not even check my driver's license.

Looking back, that was the moment when I first realized something larger was unfolding. Fanar and the man who had called me about the job were clearly operating within a world that moved by a different set of rules. What I had thought was a simple opportunity was already revealing itself to be part of a much deeper game.

Fanar filled me in on what duties would be expected of me in Iran. I would be working indirectly for the Shah. I was going to Iran working for an American company that operated in the agriculture business. The Iranian government had agricultural sites scattered all around the country, and my job would be to visit these locations, inspect the operations, and report my findings back to Tehran.

At the time, it sounded simple enough. My responsibility would be to travel from site to site, observe how the farms and facilities were operating, and document anything that needed attention. The reports would then be sent back to the officials in Tehran who oversaw the agricultural programs. I imagined long drives across unfamiliar countryside, stopping at farms and irrigation projects, talking with managers, and writing down my observations before moving on to the next location.

Iran, under the Shah, had been pushing large agricultural reforms meant to modernize farming and improve food production across the country. Many rural areas were reorganized, and new agricultural systems were introduced as part of national development efforts.

Because these projects were spread across vast regions, someone had to move between them to see what was actually happening on the ground.

Fanar explained that the work required someone who could travel easily, ask the right questions, and write clear reports. I would not be running the farms or managing the workers. My role was simply to observe and report what I saw. The way he described it made the assignment sound practical and straightforward.

As he talked, I pictured a job that involved movement and independence. There would be travel, new landscapes, and responsibilities that seemed manageable. Compared to the uncertainty I had felt just days earlier while typing my resume on the Royal typewriter, the task now sounded almost routine.

At that moment, I believed the assignment was exactly what it appeared to be. It sounded easy enough so far.

At that time in history, the Shah was the stabilizing factor in the Middle East. The United States bought much of its oil from that region, and the last thing the U.S. needed was another war or uprising in that part of the world. A calm Middle East meant steady oil and reasonable prices. In the simplest terms, a satisfied Shah helped keep the region stable. That was the way it was explained to me.

From the way Fanar described it, my role was small but useful within that larger picture. If the Shah needed something done, it had to get done. If he wanted information, someone had to gather it. The agricultural inspections were part of that structure. Reports moved upward, decisions came down, and the system kept moving.

It was presented to me in a very practical way. Travel to the sites, observe what was happening, write clear reports, and make sure the right people in Tehran knew what was going on. The smoother those operations ran, the fewer problems reached the top.

Chapter 5

Before leaving, I was told to take five thousand dollars in travelers' checks with me. That was a considerable amount of money to carry in those days, and it made the whole trip feel even more serious. I went to the bank to pick them up, thinking it would be a quick stop before finishing the rest of my preparations.

What no one told me was that every single traveler's check had to be signed by me right there in the bank.

They laid the stack in front of me and explained the process. One by one, I had to sign them, each signature matching the one I would use later when cashing them. The pile seemed to grow taller the longer I sat there, and my hand quickly began to ache from repeating the same motion over and over again.

After a while, the routine became almost mechanical. Pick up a check, sign it carefully, place it in the completed stack, and reach for the next one. By the time I was halfway through, I started wishing someone had warned me ahead of time.

I should have packed a lunch.

Getting back to the land of Richard Petty, I bought a footlocker, a new Pentax camera, packed my clothes, and then lay awake in bed most of the night. Sleep never really came. My mind kept running through the trip ahead, the places I would be going, and the things I still needed to remember before leaving. Everything was ready, though. My flight started in Greensboro and ended in Tehran, with several connecting flights along the way. On paper, it was a perfectly timed itinerary.

At least it looked perfect on paper.

Chapter 6

The next morning, I was late getting to the Greensboro airport. I arrived just in time to see my flight to Dulles pulling away from the gate as I was trying to check in. I stood there for a moment watching it disappear, already realizing what that meant for the rest of the trip.

This is where something called the domino effect comes into play.

Once the first flight is missed, everything behind it begins to fall apart. Every connection had been carefully timed. Greensboro to Dulles, Dulles to Heathrow, and Heathrow to Tehran. Each leg depended on the one before it. Missing the first one meant the rest of them were now impossible to catch.

Greensboro to Dulles, missed.

Dulles to Heathrow, missed.

Heathrow to Tehran, missed.

What had been a neatly organized travel plan only hours earlier had now collapsed in a matter of minutes. The entire chain had fallen apart before I had even left North Carolina. Standing there in the airport, watching the gate area empty out, I began to realize that my journey to Iran was already off to a much different start than the one printed on my ticket.

Still possessing the old hippie attitude, I was not about to be outdone by the "System." I went from air carrier to air carrier at each airport, trying to get my ticket reissued and my route pieced back together. What had once been a clean travel schedule had turned into what I can only describe as the itinerary from hell.

Every counter meant another explanation. Every explanation meant another hopeful look across the desk at someone who had the authority to move a seat around or stamp a ticket. I learned very quickly that persistence mattered. I moved from line to line, gate to gate, airline to airline, trying to rebuild the trip one leg at a time.

The experience turned out to be educational, even for me. I developed a skill that I had never really practiced before. I learned how to grovel, beg, and plead with ticket agents. I spoke politely, explained my situation, and tried to make them see that I truly needed to get where I was going. Surprisingly, it worked. One agent would adjust something, another would find a seat that had opened, and slowly the pieces started coming back together.

Somehow, through a combination of patience, persuasion, and a little luck, I managed to keep moving east. Each new boarding pass felt like a small victory. Airport by airport, flight by flight, the journey continued until at last the final plane carried me toward Tehran.

In the end, I made it.

I was only about a day late getting there.

Chapter 7

I arrived in the middle of the night, which meant there was no one there to meet me. There I was, a young white guy with long blond hair, standing in a large international airport, not speaking the local language, surrounded by people who clearly belonged there far more than I did. Most of the travelers and workers had darker skin and black hair, moving confidently through the building while I stood there trying to get my bearings.

It felt like I had stepped onto another planet.

Run-on sentence, I know, but that's just the way it was.

I figured I could just wait in the airport until morning and then have someone help me call the company number. That seemed like the safest and most reasonable plan. The problem was that the airport did not feel like a place where I wanted to spend the entire night. There were quite a few people wandering around who looked a little rough, and I began to get the uneasy feeling that staying there might not be the smartest decision.

So I walked outside toward the line of taxis.

It felt like a gamble, but at that moment it seemed like the better option. Thankfully, most of the cab drivers spoke at least a little English. After a few short conversations and some hand gestures, I managed to explain that it was the middle of the night and I needed a place to sleep.

One of the cabbies nodded as if he understood exactly what I meant. He loaded my footlocker into the trunk, and we pulled away from the airport into the dark streets of Tehran. The city felt unfamiliar and quiet at that hour, with only a few lights glowing in shop windows and the occasional car passing by.

After driving for a while, the cabbie stopped in front of a small restaurant that looked like it had seen better days. It was the kind of place you might pass without noticing during the day, but at that hour, it was one of the few places still open. The cab driver told me there were rooms upstairs where travelers sometimes stayed.

At that point, I was too tired to be picky.

I carried my bag inside, spoke with the man behind the counter, and arranged to rent one of the rooms above the restaurant. The room was simple and worn, but it had a bed and a door that locked, which was good enough for me.

After the long trip and the confusion of the past day, that small room felt like a safe place to stop for the night. I put my footlocker down beside the bed, stretched out, and finally allowed myself to rest, knowing that the real adventure would begin in the morning.

Chapter 8

The next morning, I got another cab and gave the driver the address of the company office. Unfortunately, he had no idea where it was. We drove around for a while, stopping now and then so he could ask people on the street, but no one seemed to recognize the address either. Eventually, he pulled over in downtown Tehran, pointed to the sidewalk, and made it clear that this was as far as he could take me.

So there I was, sitting on my footlocker on the sidewalk in the middle of Tehran, feeling somewhat homeless and probably looking like it too. People walked past, going about their morning business, while I sat there trying to figure out what my next move should be. It was one of those moments when you begin to wonder if the entire plan has fallen apart.

Then something remarkable happened.

A man who worked for the company walked past. I had met him briefly back in the States. He looked at me for a second, paused, and then recognized me. At that moment, I felt an enormous wave of relief.

There is a God.

As it turned out, the office was just around the corner from where the cab driver had dropped me off. All that wandering around the city had ended only a few steps away from where I needed to be.

We walked over to the office, and after a short round of introductions and conversation, we went out for lunch. They took me to a nearby place that served lamb kabob on a large plate of rice. Alongside the meal was a small dish of yogurt.

I had never eaten yogurt before.

Thinking it was some kind of sauce or side dish, I took a spoonful and put it in my mouth. The taste caught me completely off guard. My first thought was that it had gone bad. To me, it tasted like spoiled milk.

Without thinking, I gagged almost immediately.

The reaction was impossible to hide, and everyone at the table noticed. It took only a moment for them to realize what had happened, but by then my face was already turning red with embarrassment. They explained that yogurt was meant to be eaten with the rice and kabob, and that it was perfectly normal.

I nodded, trying to recover my dignity while quietly wishing I had known that a few seconds earlier.

He booked me a room for the night and made flight reservations for me the next day to Yazd, Iran. He also arranged for a cab to pick me up in the morning and make sure I got to the airport on time. Everything seemed to move quickly once I had finally reached the office. For them, this was all routine.

For me, it was anything but routine.

The whole culture around me was completely new. The people, the way they dressed, the food, the sounds of the city, even the rhythm of daily life, all felt unfamiliar. I had barely been in the country for a day, and already I could feel the strain of trying to absorb so many new things at once. The jet lag did not help matters either. My body still had no idea what time it was supposed to be.

That night, I tried to rest, but my mind kept replaying everything that had happened since I left home. Only a short time earlier, I had been sitting in North Carolina typing a resume on an old Royal typewriter. Now I was in Tehran, preparing to travel deeper into a country I had only recently heard I would be working in.

Chapter 9

The next morning, the cab arrived as promised and took me back to the airport. This time, the trip was smoother. I boarded a small airplane that people casually referred to as a "puddle jumper." Compared to the larger international flight that had brought me to Tehran, this one looked almost fragile. It was a small aircraft built for short regional routes.

The flight itself was quick.

Before long, we were descending toward Yazd. From the window, I could see the dry landscape stretching across the land, the colors of the desert broken here and there by the shapes of buildings and roads. When we landed, it was clear that this airport was nothing like the one in Tehran.

Yazd's airport was little more than a landing strip with a small building serving as the terminal. There were no crowds, no long corridors, and no complicated signs pointing travelers in different directions. Everything about the place felt simple and quiet.

When I stepped outside, a cab was already waiting for me. The driver looked in my direction, clearly expecting someone. It didn't take long to realize that someone was me.

Yazd. What can I say? It sat more or less in the middle of the country, a small town surrounded by desert. Vegetation was sparse. In fact, almost everything was sparse back then. The land stretched out in dusty shades of brown and tan, broken only occasionally by low buildings and the distant outline of hills. It felt quiet and remote, the kind of place where life moved at a slower pace.

I had a room waiting for me at the Safaiyeh Hotel. When we arrived, the first thing I noticed was the wall. A tall wall, easily twelve feet high, surrounded the entire property. From the outside, it looked almost fortress-like, standing alone in the middle of the desert landscape.

But once you passed through the entrance, the view changed completely.

Inside those walls was what felt like a garden of Eden. Water flowed through small channels, grass covered the ground, and palms and flowering plants filled the air with color. After seeing nothing but dry desert on the ride from the airport, the contrast was almost shocking.

The hotel itself was made up of small single bungalows scattered throughout the garden. Each room stood alone, tucked among the trees and greenery, giving the whole place a peaceful and private feeling. Walking through the grounds felt less like being at a hotel and more like wandering through a quiet oasis.

There was a restaurant on the property as well. It had some seating inside, but most of the tables were arranged outside near the pool, where people preferred to eat in the open air. The evenings were comfortable, and it was easy to sit there for hours while the warm desert air cooled after sunset.

The pool, however, was something different.

This was not one of those decorative garden pools with fountains and stone edges meant only for looks. It was clearly meant to be a swimming pool. It was large and rectangular, sitting in the middle of the courtyard area where people gathered.

Now the pool did have water in it.

But there was no diving board, and there were no ladders to climb in or out. The water also had a noticeable green tint to it, which made you wonder how often it was cleaned. Looking at it closely, I suspected that the unusual color might explain why there were no diving boards or ladders in the first place.

Chapter 10

Let's talk about cats for a minute.

Modern Iran is what used to be Persia, and Persia is famous for Persian cats. The hotel grounds seemed to be full of them. They were everywhere. They wandered through the gardens, slept under the palms, and strolled around the restaurant as if they owned the place. Most of them were beautiful animals with thick fur and calm personalities. They clearly felt at home there.

During dinner, they would often come right up to the tables. It wasn't unusual for one or two cats to jump up and sit there quietly while I ate, watching every bite with complete attention. It might have bothered some people, but I didn't mind it at all. After traveling so far and feeling so out of place, their quiet company was actually kind of comforting.

Then one day, something strange happened.

I came back from work that afternoon and immediately noticed something different. The gardens were quiet. The usual cats that lounged around the walkways and tables were nowhere to be seen. At first, I thought they were just hiding somewhere in the shade, but the longer I looked around, the more obvious it became.

Every single cat was gone.

I mean all of them.

Later that evening, I went to the restaurant for supper and opened the menu. There was a new item listed that had not been there before. Beef Stroganoff. The description said the meat was cooked in gravy, shredded, and served over a bed of rice. In Iran, almost everything seemed to be served over rice, so that part didn't surprise me.

Still, the timing crossed my mind.

All the cats had disappeared, and suddenly, there was a new shredded meat dish on the menu.

I ordered it anyway.

When the plate arrived, it looked pretty good. The meat was tender and mixed into a thick gravy, spread across a generous serving of rice. I took a bite and, honestly, it wasn't half bad. I never asked any questions about it, and no one offered any explanations.

Some things are better left alone.

The yogurt was still sitting on the side of the plate like it always was. I left it there. I could eat the cat, but the rotten milk was another matter entirely. I wasn't ready for that transition.

Chapter 11

Talking with locals and slowly finding my way around town, I eventually stumbled onto something I didn't expect to see. It was a bar. A real alcohol-serving bar. That alone surprised me. In Tehran, you might expect something like that, but out here in Yazd, in the middle of the desert, it felt completely out of place.

But there it was.

And I was not about to let that opportunity slip away.

I walked in trying to look confident, good posture, head held high, acting like I knew exactly what I was doing. The bartender looked over and gave me a short nod. I stepped up and said, "Yakie Obejo," which meant one beer. I had learned that phrase from watching Hoss order a beer on the old Ponderosa television show.

Yes, many of the popular American TV shows were shown in Iran at the time. They were all dubbed in Farsi, the language spoken in Iran. Hearing familiar characters speaking in a language that no other country seemed to use was a strange experience, but somehow it worked.

The bar itself was simple. There were no chairs and no booths, only tall tables that came up almost to chest height. Everyone stood around them while drinking and talking.

As I stood there with my drink, I took a closer look at what I had been served. Did I say beer? It was technically a bottle of homebrew. At the bottom of the bottle was about a quarter inch of thick sediment. I held the bottle very carefully, trying not to shake it or tilt it too far.

The drink had a very high alcohol content. There was no foam and no carbonation either. It was completely flat. Two bottles of that stuff and I was right where I wanted to be.

The taste was not terrible, but it was heavy and thick. The closest thing I could compare it to was slightly soapy water. Still, after the long journey and the strange days I had been having, it felt good to relax for a while.

There was one thing I learned the hard way.

Three of those beers will clean you out like a box of Xlax.

Don't ask me how I know.

Let's just say I spent the entire next morning very close to the bathroom.

Here we go again. Speaking of toilets, they had no toilets that you could actually sit down on and relax. None of the familiar porcelain seats as we had back home. Instead, what they had were holes in the floor over the sewage pipe. The first time I saw one, it reminded me of looking down a sewage manhole back in the States.

On each side of the hole, there were small places molded into the floor where you were supposed to put your feet. The idea was simple. You placed your feet on those spots, faced the wall, and then squatted.

At first, it looked like a strange system, and I was not entirely sure how well it was going to work. It took a little practice to get the balance right, especially when you were still half asleep or in a hurry. But after a while, you figured it out.

It was not comfortable in the way I was used to, and there was certainly no relaxing involved, but it did the job.

What can I say, it worked.

Chapter 12

I suppose this is the place to talk about bar food.

Every country seems to have its own version of it. The United States has wings, peanuts, and fried things. Iran had its own version, though I quickly learned it was a little different. Actually, it was a lot different.

One night, while I was standing at one of the tall tables drinking my beer, I noticed the other men in the bar eating small white cubes about an inch square. They were sitting in a white sauce on a small plate, and everyone seemed to be enjoying them. By that point, I had already learned one important lesson about food in Iran.

Sometimes it is better not to ask too many questions.

Iranians will eat just about everything on a goat, sheep, or camel. Nothing goes to waste. If it can be cooked, it will probably show up on someone's plate. So instead of asking what the dish was, I simply pointed to another man's plate and used a few hand gestures to let the barkeep know that I wanted the same thing.

He nodded, clearly understanding.

A few minutes later, he brought me a plate of the white cubes in sauce. I picked one up with my fork and tried it. To my surprise, it was actually very good. The flavor was rich, and the texture was tender. Whatever it was, I liked it.

After that, every time I stopped in for a beer, I ordered a plate of those cubes.

One day, I happened to mention the food to a friend. I told him about the bar and how good the little white cubes were. He looked at me with a grin and asked if I knew what they were made of.

I told him no.

He started laughing.

Then he explained that what I had been eating were Camel Mountain Oysters.

Well, when in Rome, do as the Romans do.

Street food is something every city and every country seems to have. Back in the United States, we love our hot dogs. You can find them on street corners, at ball games, and at roadside stands just about anywhere. It's simple food that people grab while they're on the move.

It is not that way everywhere.

In Iran, there was a street food that seemed to be sold on nearly every corner. It was called Balut. People talked about it being high in protein, and some even claimed it had certain… other benefits as well.

Balut is a boiled duck egg. But not the kind of egg you might be imagining.

The eggs are fertile and left under the hen for three to four weeks before being taken out and boiled. By that time, the duckling inside the egg has already begun to develop. It is not fully grown, but it is far beyond the simple egg stage most people are used to seeing.

When the egg is peeled, the outside still looks fairly normal. The duckling is still surrounded by the egg white, so at first glance, it resembles an ordinary boiled egg from back home.

Then you take a bite.

And that is where things become very different.

Inside the egg, you can encounter the partially formed duckling. There may be a small head, soft bones that have not hardened yet, and the faint outlines of tiny feathers. Even small blood vessels can still be present.

That was enough for me.

I tried to be polite and open-minded about the foods I encountered, but this was where I had to draw the line. The first time I saw one opened up, I immediately knew it was not something I was ready to eat.

Talk about gagging.

Over the years, I have tried it again, thinking maybe I would finally get used to it. But even now, I still cannot quite stomach it. Some experiences you just never fully adjust to.

Chapter 13

Back on the jobsite, I was assigned a car and a driver, which made getting around much easier. The company also provided me with an interpreter. He was a sixteen-year-old boy who had taken English in high school. His English skills were limited, but he did his best. He could easily say things like "Hello, how are you?" and "Good morning." Beyond that, the conversations sometimes became a little uncertain.

His name was Hussan.

Even with the language barrier, we learned to communicate fairly quickly. Much of our work involved job blueprints and specifications, and those things have a language of their own. We pointed at drawings, numbers, and measurements, using hand gestures and simple words when needed. Over time, we developed our own way of understanding each other.

One day while we were talking, Hussan said something that caught my attention. In his broken English, he told me that the Shah would soon be "no more." At first, I thought I had misunderstood him, but as I asked more questions, it became clear what he meant.

As I pressed him for more information, he explained that many ordinary people in the country held a deep resentment toward the Shah. According to him, the general working population carried a quiet but very strong dislike for the government and the way the country was being run. It was the first time I had heard anyone speak that openly about it.

Following the instructions I had been given, I included that information in my report back to Tehran.

After that report was sent, things began to change.

Soon, I started receiving requests from Tehran asking me to speak with more people and gather additional opinions. They wanted to know what workers thought, what people in town were saying, and what kind of mood existed beyond the jobsite. At first, it was simple questions, but the requests gradually became more detailed.

They even asked me to talk with people who had nothing to do with the project itself.

Each new message from Tehran asked for a little more information than the last. What had started as agricultural inspections was beginning to take on a different shape. The reports were no longer just about farms, equipment, and production. Now they were asking about conversations, attitudes, and the general feeling among the people.

And the list of questions kept growing.

Chapter 14

One afternoon at supper, sitting by the pool, I met two men wearing black suits. They were members of Savak, the Shah's personal security and intelligence force. Where I came from in North Carolina, we Tarheels would probably compare them to the FBI. The difference was that Savak had no oversight. They answered only to the Shah.

History books say that the Savak branch of the government was dissolved during the 1979 revolution. The reality was much harsher. When the revolution began, Savak offices were looted and burned. Any Savak officer who was found was dragged into the street and shot by militant groups. The anger toward them had been building for years.

The officers were one of the reasons many people disliked the Shah. I heard stories from locals about how Savak agents behaved. Some said they took whatever they wanted and intimidated anyone who questioned them. Whether every story was true or not, the fear and resentment people felt toward them was very real.

The two men in black spoke with me calmly that evening. They handed me a telex number and told me I could use it if I needed anything. By that, they meant money, instructions, or information about where I should go next and what questions I should be asking.

They wanted me to stay in touch.

Looking back on that moment, I believe that was the point when I unofficially became a Savak informant. No one said those exact words, but the meaning was clear enough.

I did not own a telex machine, but they told me where a few of them were located around town. Most of them were hidden away in the basements of office buildings where business communications were handled. After asking around, I eventually found a man who was willing to send telex messages for me.

Whenever I needed to send something to Tehran or back to the United States, I would bring the message to him. He would type it into the machine and send it along the network. For his trouble, I paid him a few rials each time.

It was a simple arrangement, but it worked.

It was important for me to remember where everything was, just in case I needed it later, either for myself or for someone else. While moving around the area, I began noticing the different facilities and equipment scattered across the region.

One place in particular caught my attention.

There was a large hammer mill not far from the jobsite. A hammer mill is used to break large kernels of corn into smaller pieces, usually for animal feed. Since I was working in what was supposed to be the agriculture business, I also knew where large amounts of corn were stored. Corn was easy to come by, and so were other things like sugar and yeast, which could be bought almost anywhere in town.

After thinking about it for a while, I began to see a possible business opportunity.

I mentioned the idea to a few expatriate country boys who were also working in the area. They were the kind of fellows who grew up around farms and understood certain processes without needing long explanations. When I brought it up, they immediately understood what I was getting at.

Say no more. They already knew what to do, how to do it, and where it could be done.

Before long, we had ourselves a small arrangement. My part was simple. I would get the corn delivered to the hammer mill so it could be processed. When the grinding was finished, the mill operator would contact the boys and let them know the material was ready to pick up. I also supplied the sugar and yeast that were needed.

The rest of the work was handled by them.

They had pressure cookers that were used during their part of the process. I never got involved with that end of it. I didn't ask questions, and I didn't need to see how they handled things. My role was simply to connect the pieces and keep the supplies moving.

In other words, I was just the middleman.

Chapter 15

The Arabs and Iranians liked the moonshine well enough, but gin was really their drink of choice. Gin has a very distinct taste, almost like taking a mouthful of juniper berries. That flavor is what sets it apart from other kinds of alcohol.

Being the creative group that we were, we started thinking about how to work around that. One of the guys suggested having someone bring a bag of juniper berries from the States on their next trip over. It sounded simple enough, and before long, that's exactly what happened.

When the bag arrived, we put the juniper berries into a cotton sack and dropped them into the moonshine. We let it sit and soak for a while so the flavor would seep into the alcohol.

Just like that, we had something that passed for gin.

It wasn't perfect, but it was close enough. Once the juniper flavor settled into the liquor, the taste changed enough that people recognized it as gin. For the customers we had, that was all that mattered.

Word spread quickly among the expatriates and locals who were looking for a drink. Before long, we could hardly keep up with the demand. A single bottle sold for about a hundred dollars, which was serious money at the time.

And the most surprising part was how quickly it disappeared.

Every bottle we produced sold almost as soon as it was ready.

OK, I'm getting off track here.

Around this time, I began to realize that my simple "inspect and report" job was slowly putting me in the kind of position people describe as being caught between a rock and a hard place. Working for Savak, even unofficially, had its own set of complications. The more information I passed along, the more involved I seemed to become. Looking back, it felt like one of those situations that quietly grows bigger while you are busy dealing with the day-to-day details.

That seems to be the story of my life.

Not long after that, the Buin Zahra project needed to be "tweaked," so I was sent there for about a week. The area had a small setup for the expatriate workers. There was a modest duplex where the expats stayed, and I was given a bed there while I worked on the site.

The place was simple but comfortable enough.

There was also a houseboy assigned to the duplex. His name was Sergei. Despite the title, he was not really a boy at all. I would guess he was around thirty-five years old. Sergei was Russian and spoke very little English, though he managed to communicate well enough to get the daily work done.

I often suspected that he might also be connected to Savak in some way, quietly keeping an eye on the expatriates who came and went from the project. That was just my impression. In those days, it sometimes felt like someone was always watching.

Sergei handled most of the day-to-day chores around the duplex. He cooked lunch and supper for the crew and kept the place clean. The meals were simple but filling, usually centered around rice, meat, and whatever vegetables were available.

The duplex also had a washing machine, something that was fairly common to Americans but completely new to Sergei. It was an electric washing machine, the kind you simply loaded, turned on, and let run.

Sergei found it fascinating.

Whenever the washer was running, he would stand beside it and watch it work. Every few minutes, he would lift the lid and look inside as if checking to see what it was doing. Then he would close the lid again and continue watching.

He did this every time the machine was used.

I never did figure out exactly what he was expecting to see in there.

Chapter 16

One afternoon when I came in from the project, the duplex was filled with the smell of something wonderful cooking on the stove. After a long day at the site, that kind of smell had a way of getting your attention right away. It drifted through the whole place, rich and savory, the kind of aroma that makes you instantly hungry.

On the stove was a large pot with a lid sitting over a steady flame. Whatever Sergei was cooking had clearly been simmering for a while. Curious to see what we were having for supper, I walked over and lifted the lid.

The pot was about three-quarters full of broth.

But staring straight up at me from the middle of the pot was a sheep's head. Eyeballs and all.

For a moment, I just stood there looking at it. The head was fully intact, floating in the liquid, its expression frozen in a way that made it feel like it was looking right back at me. It was not quite the surprise I had expected when I lifted that lid.

Sergei came into the room a few seconds later and seemed perfectly pleased with what was cooking. For him, it was just another meal being prepared the way he had probably seen it done his entire life.

Supper that night was definitely different.

As I sat there staring at the bowl in front of me, I found myself thinking about all the foods I had already encountered since arriving in Iran. In that moment, I even started to reconsider my earlier opinion about yogurt.

It suddenly didn't seem so bad after all.

The American agriculture company eventually opened an office in Isfahan, and I was transferred there. With the move came a few changes. For one thing, I stepped away from the bootlegging business and left that operation to the country boys who had been running most of it anyway. They knew the process well by that point and didn't need me around to keep things moving.

The company arranged a place for me to live once I arrived. They rented me a flat on a hill that the expatriates in the area had nicknamed "Jack-Ass Hill." I never learned the official name of the place, but everyone seemed to know it by that nickname. The hill overlooked parts of the city and caught a steady breeze most afternoons, which made it a comfortable place to stay.

Along with the apartment, the office also gave me a car. This time, there was no driver assigned. I would be getting myself around from now on.

The car was a Mehari, built by the French company Citroën. It was somewhat similar to the Volkswagen vehicle known as "The Thing," a simple, rugged car designed more for practicality than style. The Mehari had a small two-cylinder gasoline engine and a three-speed manual transmission.

The gear shift was unlike anything I had ever seen before. Instead of coming up through the floor, it stuck straight out of the dashboard. Then it made a ninety-degree turn upward where the shift knob sat. The shifting process was a combination of pulling, turning, and pushing the lever into place. It took a little getting used to, but after a short while, it felt completely natural.

The car itself was open with no doors and no roof. It had a very basic, almost military look to it. Everything about it was simple and functional.

And I loved that little car.

Once I got comfortable with it, I drove it everywhere.

Chapter 17

Isfahan had a large military presence at the time, and the United States supported much of the equipment and training there. There were quite a few Americans living in the city, many of them working on or around the military base. Contractors, technicians, and advisors had come from the States to support the Shah's modernization programs and the growing Iranian military.

The expatriates played an important role in keeping the equipment running. A lot of the aircraft and helicopters Iran had purchased from the United States required trained mechanics and instructors. American technicians helped maintain the helicopters and also trained Iranian pilots and crew members so they could eventually operate the machines themselves.

You could see the results of that cooperation around Isfahan. American workers moved through the city alongside Iranians who were learning the trade. The base had a steady flow of activity, with aircraft maintenance, flight training, and technical instruction all happening at the same time.

For many of the Americans living there, the job was fairly straightforward. Their responsibility was to keep the helicopters flying, teach the Iranians how to fly them, and maintain them properly. It was part of the larger relationship between the United States and the Shah's government during that period, when Iran was one of Washington's closest allies in the region before the revolution changed everything.

In Isfahan, that meant there were always plenty of Americans around town. Some were military advisors, some were engineers, and others were contractors working on aviation projects. For a while, the city had a surprisingly large expatriate community, all tied in one way or another to the work being done at the base.

Which brings me to another matter. The Shah often appeared to have no real enemies at the time, at least not in the open. Yet he was constantly purchasing military equipment from the United States. Jets, helicopters, and even large naval vessels for the Persian Gulf seemed to be arriving one after another.

To someone like me, watching from the outside, it sometimes felt excessive. Iran already had a strong military presence in the region, and the steady stream of new hardware made you wonder what the long-term plan really was. The Shah had enormous oil revenue to work with, and much of that money went into building one of the most modern armed forces in the Middle East.

American companies benefited from those purchases, and American advisors and technicians were everywhere helping maintain the equipment and train the Iranian crews. The relationship between the two countries was very close during that period, and the military cooperation reflected that.

Still, from time to time, I found myself asking a simple question.

Was I working for a man who simply never had enough toys to play with as a child?

It was an odd thought, but watching the steady buildup of aircraft, helicopters, and ships sometimes made it feel that way.

Go figure.

Chapter 18

There was a job start-up in Mashhad that I needed to be on. I had to be there Monday morning, and unfortunately, it happened to fall during an Iranian holiday weekend. Every flight was booked. Every train was full. Even the buses were packed with travelers trying to get across the country.

That left me with only one real option.

I had to drive.

So there I was, heading out in my little Mehari, pointing the nose of that open French car toward the Caspian mountains. On paper, it sounded like a terrible idea. A small two-cylinder car, no roof, no doors, and a long trip across mountain roads in a country I was still learning how to navigate.

I complained about it, of course. Anyone would.

But the truth is, I loved it.

The drive took me through some of the most dramatic scenery I had ever seen. The desert landscapes slowly gave way to rising hills, and before long, the road began climbing through the mountains. The air cooled as the elevation increased, and the views stretched for miles in every direction. Small villages appeared along the road, with farmers, roadside markets, and people going about their daily lives.

Driving that little car through the mountains felt like an adventure all by itself.

The Mehari bounced along happily, its tiny engine working hard but never complaining. With no roof over my head and the wind moving through the car, the whole trip felt wide open and free in a way you rarely experience anymore.

What had started as a problem turned into one of the best drives I ever made.

Sometimes the only way to get somewhere is the long way around. And every once in a while, that ends up being the best way to travel.

There was a German company that had some equipment on that job that needed a technician to do the start-up. They were in the same situation we were in. No flights, no trains, and no buses because of the holiday weekend. Someone from their office asked if their technician could ride with me.

That was fine with me.

His name was Marten. He was about my age and had that unmistakable British manner about him. Easygoing, polite, and always ready for a beer. It didn't take long for the two of us to get along.

So Marten and I did what we thought was the most sensible thing anyone could do before heading out on a long drive across the mountains.

We bought a cooler, filled it with ice, packed it full of German beer, and pointed the Mehari toward the east with Tehran somewhere behind us.

Well, that's the romantic version of the story anyway.

Just kidding about watching Tehran disappear in the rear-view mirror. The Mehari didn't have one.

Chapter 19

As the evening turned into night, the road through the mountains became darker and quieter. The little car kept moving along, but those headlights were about the size of flashlights and didn't light up much more than the road directly in front of us. Between the winding mountain roads, the long day of travel, and the steady supply of beer from the cooler, we started to feel the wear and tear of the trip.

The farther we drove, the more tired we became.

Finally, we both came to the same conclusion at about the same time.

We pulled the car off to the side of the road and decided to get some sleep. The mountains were quiet, the night air was cool, and after the long drive, the idea of resting for a while sounded just fine to me.

A couple of hours later I woke up to the sound of a truck engine nearby. When I opened my eyes, there was a 1970s deuce-and-a-half military transport parked beside us. The truck was full of armed soldiers, and several of them were standing outside looking down at the two of us sleeping next to the road.

They were clearly trying to tell us something.

At first, it sounded like they were scolding us. They kept repeating that we could not park there. I didn't understand the problem. It was the middle of the night, there was no traffic anywhere, and we were not blocking the road.

Why would it matter if we slept there for a few hours?

Between their broken English and the small amount of Farsi Marten and I had picked up, we slowly began to understand what they were trying to tell us.

They kept saying one word over and over.

Wolves.

At first, I thought I had misunderstood them, but they made it clear enough with gestures and a few extra words. They were warning us that wolves roamed the mountains in that area. According to them, wolves sometimes attacked people who became stranded along the road at night.

Apparently, it happened more often than we would have guessed.

Once that message finally sank in, both Marten and I were suddenly very awake. Sleeping in the car no longer sounded like such a good idea.

The soldiers were not being unfriendly at all. In fact, they were doing us a favor by stopping to warn us before something unpleasant happened.

Looking back on that moment, I remember thinking one simple thing.

See, I told you there was a God.

Everything went smoothly on the job start-up in Meshad. The best I remember, Marten flew back to Isfahan, and I drove. The road stretched ahead for miles, cutting through dry mountain passes before gradually opening into greener country as I moved closer to the north. After the long hours behind the wheel, the quiet rhythm of the drive gave me time to unwind from the intensity of the work we had just finished.

At one point along the route, I stopped at a very nice restaurant overlooking the Caspian Sea and indulged in a meal of smoked sturgeon. It was not something I had ever tried before, and curiosity alone was enough to convince me to order it. The fish had a rich, smoky flavor that was unlike anything I had tasted back home.

Sitting there with the sea in view and the salty air drifting in from the water made the meal feel even more memorable after the long trip.

The whole restaurant atmosphere was different and not what I was used to. The place felt calm and well-organized, and everything seemed to move at a slower and more relaxed pace. The dining room had large windows facing the water, and the light from the late afternoon sun reflected across the sea and into the room. There was a quiet sense of refinement in the way the place was run, something that immediately stood out to me.

The waiters spoke good English and were extremely polite and welcoming. They took their time explaining the menu and seemed genuinely interested in making sure I enjoyed the meal. That level of attentiveness was not something I had experienced often while traveling, and it made the stop feel less like a quick roadside meal and more like a proper break in the journey.

I believe the Europeans vacation on the Caspian every year, and that may have been what made the difference. The restaurant had the feeling of a place accustomed to international travelers. The service, the menu, and the overall atmosphere seemed designed with visitors in mind. Sitting there for a while, watching the quiet movement of the water and the occasional boats in the distance, I could easily understand why people would choose to spend their holidays along that coast.

After finishing the meal, I lingered a little longer than I had planned, enjoying the calm before continuing the drive. Eventually, I settled the bill, thanked the staff, and headed back to the car. The road still had many miles ahead of me, but the stop by the Caspian Sea had broken up the journey in a way that made the rest of the trip feel much easier.

Chapter 20

On the drive back to Isfahan, I decided to stop at a small roadside dive for breakfast. The sun had barely climbed above the horizon, and the road had been quiet for miles, so the little place caught my attention right away. It looked simple and worn, the kind of place travelers stop when they just need something warm to eat and a moment to sit down before getting back on the road.

Inside, there was a young kid behind the grill, and no one else in the place. The room was small and plain, with only a few tables scattered around and the faint smell of cooking oil hanging in the air. A small radio was playing somewhere in the background, though it was quiet enough that the sound of the grill heating up was easier to notice. The kid looked up when I walked in, but did not say much, just waited to see what I would do.

I just wanted some eggs for breakfast, nothing complicated, but ordering them turned out to be a bit of a challenge. I started trying to explain in my broken Farsi what I was hoping for. My vocabulary was limited at best, so I relied heavily on hand gestures and the universal motions people use when they are describing food. I pointed at the grill, held up two fingers, and tried to piece together the right words, the best I could remember them.

The kid let me go on like that for a few minutes. I must have looked ridiculous standing there, half-talking and half-acting out my request with my hands. Every now and then, he nodded politely, but he never interrupted. I kept trying different words, repeating myself, and hoping something I said would make sense.

Finally, he stopped me and said, in perfect English, "You want two scrambled eggs and buttered toast, is that all?"

For a moment, I just stood there and stared at him. After all that effort trying to explain myself, he had understood exactly what I wanted the whole time. The way he said it was calm and matter-of-fact, as if there had never been any confusion at all.

I laughed, nodded, and told him that was exactly right.

You just gotta' love'em.

After things got back to normal, if there was such a thing, my counterpart Phillip, who was also a Tarheel working in Saudi, flew over to see our Isfahan operation. By that point, life had settled into a routine again, at least as much as it ever did in that part of the world. Work moved forward, equipment was running, and the daily pressures of the job had replaced the earlier uncertainty.

Phillip and I had known each other for a while, and when he came through Isfahan, we spent some time catching up. It was good to see a familiar face and talk with someone who understood the strange rhythm of working overseas. We sat around one afternoon talking about work, the company, and the usual stories that seem to surface whenever two Americans find themselves a long way from home.

During the conversation, the subject came up about "the man behind the desk," the one who always seemed to know more than anyone else about what was going on. I mentioned how he seemed to know quite a lot about me personally, things that I had never told him directly. It had always struck me as a little unusual, though I had never pressed the issue.

Phillip just leaned back and laughed.

That reaction caught my attention right away. I asked him what was so funny, and he simply said that he knew exactly what I was talking about. According to Phillip, the company had been keeping tabs on me for quite some time. Apparently, I had been on their radar for a couple of years before I ever realized it.

He told me they had a full background on me. Not just my recent work history, but details going all the way back to my time in the military academy. They knew where I had trained, where I had worked, and probably more than a few things I had forgotten myself. Phillip said it as if it were no big deal, just part of how large international companies sometimes operated.

Hearing that left me a little surprised. I had always assumed they knew the basics about my professional experience, but the idea that they had been following my path for years was something else entirely. It made me wonder when exactly I had first caught their attention and what it was about my background that made them keep track of me.

Why they did it, I never really learned. To this day I do not know whether they were simply watching for potential hires, keeping a list of people with certain skills, or if there was some other reason entirely. All I know is that somewhere along the way, long before I ever set foot in Isfahan, someone had been paying attention.

Chapter 21

Back to the political environment. The American Embassy in Tehran issued a statement to the expats that it might be wise for non-essential personnel to head home. The message circulated quickly through the expatriate community. Word traveled from one job site to another, from office conversations to late-night phone calls between Americans scattered across the country. Everyone had heard something, though no one seemed to know exactly how serious it really was.

I read the statement to mean family members, tourists, and the like. People who were not directly tied to the operations that kept things running. At the time, many of us working there believed our presence was still necessary. The projects were ongoing, the equipment needed to be maintained, and the companies we worked for had made large commitments in the region. Leaving suddenly did not seem like a realistic option.

Looking back, the wording of that message was careful. It was not a direct order, and it was not an evacuation notice. It sounded more like cautious advice. I think the Embassy was trying to stay low-key and avoid creating panic. They likely did not want to publicly challenge the Shah's authority or send a signal that the situation had already passed the point of control. Diplomacy tends to move carefully, even when events on the ground are moving fast.

At the same time, those of us who had been watching the mood of the country shift could sense that something was changing. Demonstrations had become more frequent, conversations in the streets felt different, and the general tension in the air was hard to ignore. Still, it is easy to convince yourself that things will settle down tomorrow, especially when you are in the middle of work and daily routines.

My interpretation of the message was simple. I assumed it applied to people who could easily leave without disrupting anything important. Workers like me believed we were expected to stay and keep things running. In hindsight, it may have also been a subtle way of telling the rest of us that it was time to get the hell outta' Dodge without saying it outright.

I did not listen.

From that point forward, things began to move in a direction that was impossible to ignore. Each day seemed to bring another sign that the situation was getting worse. The atmosphere grew heavier, and the uncertainty that had once felt distant started creeping into everyday life. It went downhill from that day forward.

A short time after that I was walking from the office, wearing my jacket, heading back up to my flat. It was an ordinary walk that I had made many times before, the same streets and the same small shops along the way. Then suddenly everything changed. Car horns began blaring all around me, one after another, and people started shouting in the streets. The noise seemed to come from every direction at once, and it was clear something big had just happened.

I stopped at the little pizza shop along the way to see what was going on. The place was small, and a few people were gathered inside, all talking at once and trying to understand the news. Someone finally said it plainly. The Shah had left the country. Not just stepped away for a trip or a meeting somewhere, but gone. Exiled.

The atmosphere shifted immediately. The shouting outside grew louder, and the horns kept sounding. Some people seemed excited, others angry, and the streets suddenly felt very different from the way they had only minutes before. It was the kind of moment when you realize history has just taken a sharp turn.

Now I still had another quarter mile to walk to get back to my flat, and the streets between me and there were filled with locals. Many of them were already angry, and a lot of that anger was aimed squarely at America. Standing there, it became very clear that I looked exactly like what I was. If I did not look American, no one did.

So I pulled up my hoodie and cinched it down tight to cover as much of my blond hair as I could. I kept my head low and decided to take a back street instead of the main road. The walk suddenly felt much longer than it actually was. Every step made me more aware of the tension building around me.

When I finally made it back to the flat, the situation was already changing quickly. The American office in Isfahan would be vacated the following day. Everyone who worked there would be gone. Plans had already been made for them to leave.

They did not take me with them. I never understood that.

Standing there alone, the realization slowly settled in. The support system I had relied on was disappearing overnight. The people I worked with were leaving, and the office that had been the center of our operations would soon be empty.

For the first time since arriving there, I started feeling like a lone wolf without a pack. I was on my own.

Still, I made up my mind right then that I was going to get through it. No matter how uncertain things were becoming, I was determined to find my way out of the situation and keep moving forward.

Horns blew all night, gunshots rang out, and tracers filled the air. It sounded like a battlefield, but in truth, it was a celebration. People filled the streets, shouting and firing weapons into the air. The city did not sleep that night. From my flat, I could hear the constant noise echoing through the streets, sometimes distant and sometimes close enough to make you pause and listen.

Chapter 22

When the Shah left, the military laid their guns down. Rather than holding the line, many soldiers simply handed their weapons over to the militants and disappeared into the crowds. Authority had dissolved almost overnight. Whatever structure had been holding the country together seemed to vanish with him, leaving a vacuum that was quickly being filled by people with rifles and a lot of anger.

It was time for me to do some serious personal soul-searching and planning. The situation was changing faster than anyone could keep up with, and the reality was beginning to sink in. I was alone in a country that was rapidly turning hostile toward Americans, and the normal channels that might have helped me were gone.

All the urban airports in the country had been shut down. Flights had stopped, and travel was being restricted everywhere. The only airport still operating was in Tehran. That was also where the American Embassy was located, which meant it had become the only realistic exit point for anyone trying to leave the country.

My problem was distance. Tehran was roughly three hundred miles away.

All of my normal contacts had disappeared. Some had already left, some had gone into hiding, and others simply could not be reached anymore. The network of people that had once made working there manageable had dissolved almost overnight.

Fortunately, I still had one Iranian friend who was willing to help. He contacted the Embassy in Tehran to see if he could learn anything about what was happening. Information was scarce, but he managed to get through and ask about the situation.

The answer was both encouraging and urgent.

He was told that Pan Am was bringing in five Boeing 737s to evacuate Americans from Tehran. They were preparing to move as many people out of the country as they could.

The message was simple.

All I had to do was get to Tehran.

I did have some civilian Iranian friends who were willing to help me. In a situation where many people had disappeared or gone silent, that kind of loyalty meant a lot. They knew the risks, but they were still willing to stand beside me and help me get out of the country.

The problem was that we did not know when Pan Am would arrive in Tehran or how long the evacuation flights would continue. There was no clear timeline and no reliable communication coming out of the Embassy. For all we knew, the planes might arrive the next day, or they might already be on their way. Time had suddenly become the most uncertain part of the equation.

I also had friends in Tehran who were willing to take me in for a while if I could make it there. Their plan was simple. I could stay with them quietly until the evacuation flights began. When Pan Am finally started moving Americans out of the country, I would head for the airport and try to get on one of those planes.

There was another option as well. My Iranian friends in Isfahan were willing to drive me south to Bandar on the Persian Gulf. From there, I could try to catch a fishing boat across the water to Bahrain. Once in Bahrain, I could walk straight into the American Embassy and turn myself in. It would not have been comfortable or easy, but it would have taken me out of the middle of the unrest.

So I had two choices in front of me. One road led north to Tehran, where the evacuation flights were supposed to happen. The other road led south to the Gulf and the possibility of slipping quietly out of the country by boat.

Looking back now, the safer route might have been the one toward Bahrain. It would have avoided the crowds, the demonstrations, and the growing hostility that was building in the cities. But at the time, the Embassy in Tehran seemed like the most direct path out.

I am not known for making great decisions, so I chose the Tehran route.

As it turned out, that choice proved once again exactly what I was known for.

Another questionable decision.

Chapter 23

You have seen the TV news reports where they show streets blocked with overturned cars and piles of burning tires meant to keep unwanted people from passing through. Scenes like that are often hard to believe when you are watching them on a screen, but they are very real in certain parts of the world. At that time, it was real life in every town between Isfahan and Tehran. There was no toll road to bypass the trouble and no highway that allowed you to slip around the cities. The road went straight through them.

That meant every mile of the trip carried a certain amount of uncertainty. Each town had its own crowds, its own mood, and its own groups of people deciding who could pass and who could not. There was no predicting what we would run into next.

There were only two of us in the car, the driver and I sitting in the back seat. He knew the roads, and he understood the local situation much better than I did. I kept quiet and tried to stay out of sight as much as possible. Sitting in the back made it easier for me to stay low if we came up on a group that might not be happy to see an American face.

The car itself was nothing special, just a small vehicle that blended in with the traffic moving along the road. That was exactly what we wanted. Drawing attention was the last thing either of us needed on a trip like this.

The only things I had with me were my passport, my plane ticket, and some British pounds in my pocket. Everything else had been left behind. There was no luggage, no spare clothing, nothing that would slow us down or raise questions if someone decided to look inside the car.

I was already starting to feel hungry, but that was the least of my concerns. Food could wait. Right now, the only thing that mattered was getting to Tehran.

We still had about three hundred miles to go. Three hundred miles of uncertain roads, unpredictable checkpoints, and towns that might or might not let us pass through.

I leaned back in the seat and tried to keep my mind focused on the one thought that mattered.

Think positive. We can do this.

Chapter 24

About this time was when Ayatollah Ruhollah Khomeini, who had been exiled by the Shah many years earlier, decided it was time to return to Iran. He had spent years outside the country, first in Iraq and later in France, after opposing the Shah's government. When the Shah finally left Iran in January 1979, the path was open for Khomeini to come back and take control of the revolution.

He arrived in Tehran on February 1, 1979, flying in from Paris on a chartered Air France jet. Millions of people flooded the streets to welcome him home, treating his return almost like the arrival of a victorious leader. The crowds were so large that his motorcade could barely move through the city.

For people already inside the country, the atmosphere changed overnight.

More partying in the streets. More horns blowing. More gunshots are echoing across the cities. The crowds seemed to multiply everywhere. Demonstrations turned into celebrations, and celebrations turned into something that felt far less predictable. Militants appeared in greater numbers, many of them carrying weapons that had only recently been in the hands of the military.

Every day, the streets seemed fuller, louder, and more intense than the day before. What had started as political unrest was turning into something far bigger, something that was clearly reshaping the entire country.

And for anyone trying to quietly leave Iran at that moment, the situation had just become a lot more complicated.

We had to get food on the way to Tehran as well as gas, and somehow make it through the blockades. Every town seemed to have its own group of militants controlling the road. During the Iranian Revolution, crowds, armed groups, and makeshift checkpoints became common as government authority collapsed and revolutionary factions took control of streets and highways.

My driver handled most of the talking whenever we rolled up to one of those checkpoints. Each time the militants stepped toward the car with their rifles slung over their shoulders, he calmly told them that I was French. Apparently, that sounded better than telling them the truth.

For a while, that story worked.

They would look into the car, ask a few questions, glance around, and then wave us through. Each time we drove away, I felt the tension in the car slowly release, at least until we saw the next roadblock ahead in the distance.

Then we came to one checkpoint where things did not go so smoothly.

One of the militants stepped forward and asked to see my passport. There was no way around that request. My driver tried talking his way past it, but the man was not interested in explanations. He wanted to see the document.

The moment he opened it, the jig was up.

The mood around the car changed instantly. The men standing there were suddenly very angry. Being an American at that moment in Iran was about the worst thing you could be. The revolution had turned a lot of people against the United States, and emotions were running high everywhere.

They started shouting and arguing with my driver. I kept quiet and did the only thing that seemed smart at the time. I stood there with my head down and let him handle it.

My driver stepped in front of me and began running interference, talking fast and trying to calm them down. I could not understand everything he was saying, but I could hear the urgency in his voice. He was trying to convince them that I was not a problem and that we should be allowed to continue on our way.

All I could do was stand there and wait to see how it was going to end.

There were no gas stations out in the desert, at least not the kind we were used to. No bright signs, no rows of pumps, no convenience store inside selling coffee and sandwiches. Fuel stops along those roads were much simpler than that.

Every now and then, we would come across a man sitting beside the road with a fifty-five-gallon drum full of gasoline. A small hand pump would be attached to the barrel, and that was the entire operation. If you needed fuel, that was where you stopped.

The price was whatever you could negotiate. There was no posted rate and no receipt waiting at the end. A short conversation would take place, sometimes a little bargaining, and eventually both sides would settle on a number that seemed acceptable.

Then the real process began.

The hose on the pump would never reach the car. It was always just a little too short. That meant the man would start pumping gas into a five-gallon can instead. Once the can was full, it would be carried over to the car and carefully poured into the tank.

Then the whole thing started again.

Pump the gas into the can.

Carry the can to the car.

Pour it into the tank.

Repeat.

Chapter 25

It was slow and a little messy, but it was the only way to keep moving across those long stretches of road. When you were trying to travel three hundred miles across a country in the middle of a revolution, you did not complain about the method. You were just grateful that someone was sitting there with a barrel of fuel.

The quaint little town of Qom, the home of Khomeini and one of the major religious centers in Iran, was tough to get through. The city had already played an important role in the uprising that eventually became the Iranian Revolution, with protests there helping ignite demonstrations across the country.

By the time we reached it, the streets were packed and tense. Every road seemed to be blocked. People had dragged tires into the middle of the streets and set them on fire, building black walls of smoke and flame that forced traffic to slow to a crawl. Cars, trucks, and whatever else they could find were used to choke off the roads. There was no simple way around it.

I am convinced there are no spare tires left in that town. It felt like every tire in Qom had been dragged out into the street and set on fire. The thick smoke hung low over the roads, and the heat from the burning piles pushed everyone farther back from the barricades.

Our driver had to ease the car slowly from one gap to the next, trying to find openings where the roadblocks were not completely sealed off. Sometimes the crowds would move aside just enough to let a vehicle creep through. Other times, we had to circle around and try a different street.

Every minute inside that town felt longer than the last. The noise, the shouting, the smoke from the burning tires, and the constant movement of people made the whole place feel like it was boiling over.

Getting through Qom was not just another stretch of road on the trip to Tehran. It felt like running a gauntlet.

They searched the car, searched the driver and me, and interrogated both of us. It felt like the questions went on forever. Men circled the car, opening doors, checking under seats, looking into every corner they could reach. They went through our pockets, asked where we had come from, where we were going, and why we were traveling. I never did find out exactly what they were looking for. Maybe they did not know either. Eventually, they seemed satisfied, or at least tired of questioning us, and they waved us on.

Getting fuel for the car was still a problem, and finding something to eat was not much easier. But by then, that had become part of the routine. Every stop required patience and a little luck. The road was unpredictable, and supplies were scattered wherever someone happened to be selling them. At the time, it all seemed like just another day on the road crossing the desert during the middle of a revolution.

Looking back now, the fact that I thought any of that was normal says something about how long I had stayed in that environment. When you live inside chaos long enough, the unusual begins to feel ordinary.

The trip to Tehran took more than two full days. The distance itself was not impossible, but the checkpoints, roadblocks, and constant questioning slowed everything down. Each town had its own group of militants controlling the roads, and every one of them wanted answers before letting us pass.

Even when we finally reached the outskirts of Tehran, the trouble was not over. The militants did not want to let us into the interior of the city. More interrogations followed, along with the usual hassles and delays that had become part of the journey. Somehow, little by little, we managed to move closer to the center of the city.

Eventually, I made it to the safe house.

Walking through that door felt like stepping into a different world. After days of uncertainty and tension on the road, it was good to be among my own people again. Familiar voices, familiar faces, and the simple comfort of knowing you were not alone anymore made a big difference.

Chapter 26

Outside, the city was still in full celebration. The militants following Khomeini in Tehran seemed to party every night and every day. Gunfire echoed through the streets, horns blared constantly, and crowds moved through the city in a kind of nonstop celebration. For them, it was the beginning of something new. For those of us trying to leave the country, it was just another reminder that the situation was far from over.

The Embassy called. The first evacuation flight would be tomorrow, but they did not have a timeline yet. Everything was still uncertain, and the situation in the city was changing by the hour. They told me that if I wanted to come down to the Embassy that evening, I could stay there overnight and take the Embassy bus to the airport in the morning.

On the surface, it sounded simple enough. Just make my way across Tehran, spend the night at the Embassy, and catch the bus with the other Americans heading to the airport. After everything I had just gone through to reach the city, the offer almost sounded too easy.

And when something sounds too good to be true, it usually is.

Tehran at that moment was not exactly a calm place to move around in the middle of the night. The streets were still filled with crowds celebrating the revolution. Militants were everywhere, checkpoints were scattered across the city, and gunfire could still be heard echoing through different neighborhoods. Just getting across town safely was not guaranteed.

Still, the Embassy was the official route out of the country. If I could make it there, I would be with other Americans and under some level of protection. The idea of riding a bus with them directly to the airport sounded a lot better than trying to find my own way through the chaos again the next morning.

But experience had already taught me something during that trip.

Nothing in that country was going to be easy anymore.

Chapter 27

February 14, 1979.

Happy Valentine's Day, lol.

My friends called a cab for me to take me to the Embassy. By that point, the city had settled into a strange rhythm of celebration, tension, and uncertainty. People were still in the streets, horns were still blowing from time to time, and the atmosphere carried that same restless energy that had been building for days.

The cab driver showed up, but it did not take long for him to make it clear that he knew something was happening in that part of town. The Embassy area was becoming a place people preferred to avoid. Too many foreigners, too much attention, and too many militants nearby watching who came and went.

As we drove through the city, he kept glancing around, clearly uncomfortable with where we were headed. Finally, he told me that he was not going to stop directly at the entrance gate to the Embassy. He said he would drive a little farther down the block, let me out there, and I would have to walk back to the gate on my own.

For some reason, that did not bother me at all.

By then, I had been dealing with strange situations for days. Roadblocks, interrogations, burning tires, gunfire in the streets, and two days of driving across the country had shifted my sense of what counted as normal. Getting dropped off a block away from the Embassy barely registered as unusual.

The cab finally slowed down and pulled over a short distance from the compound. I stepped out, paid the driver, and watched him drive away without hesitation. He clearly had no interest in lingering anywhere near that place.

Then I started walking back toward the Embassy gate.

Looking back on it now, my reaction says a lot about how much that environment had already changed my thinking. When chaos becomes routine, even odd situations start to feel ordinary.

I think the term we use today for that kind of moment is simple.

Whatever.

So far, so good. I made it through the gate, saw a lot of familiar and relieved faces, and checked in with the man in charge at the Embassy. There were Americans everywhere, some sitting quietly, others talking in low voices, everyone trying to figure out what was going to happen next. Just being inside the compound felt like a small victory after everything it had taken to get there.

The man in charge told me the Embassy bus would leave early in the morning for the airport. That was the plan. The evacuation flights were expected to begin, and the bus would take everyone straight out to the airport, where the Pan Am planes were supposed to pick us up.

He did not have any beds available, though. The place was already crowded with people who had arrived earlier, all trying to get out of the country just like I was. He told me I could sleep anywhere I could find space to lay my head. A couch, a chair, the floor, it did not matter. At that point, none of us was too concerned about comfort.

Chapter 28

After two days on the road, even a hard floor inside the Embassy walls sounded pretty good to me.

For a short while, things seemed calm. People were settling in for the night, some talking quietly about their own journeys getting there, others simply trying to rest while they could. There was a sense that we had finally reached a place of safety, that the hardest part might already be behind us.

Then everything changed.

It was about that time that the militants made their first assault on the Embassy. Within moments, the calm feeling inside the compound disappeared. The noise outside grew louder, shouting could be heard beyond the walls, and it quickly became clear that the situation was no longer under control.

Before long, the militants had forced their way in and taken over the Embassy.

The place that had seemed like a safe haven only minutes earlier had suddenly become something very different.

The militants came in behind a wall of women and children. They knew exactly what they were doing. Our few soldiers guarding the Embassy would never fire into a crowd like that, especially with women and kids standing in front. It was a tactic that removed any real chance of resistance before the confrontation even began.

The Embassy guards could see what was happening and understood the situation immediately. There simply were not enough of them, and the way the crowd was being used made it impossible to respond with force. Instead of trying to fight a battle they could not win, they shifted their focus to protecting what they could inside the building.

Two of the soldiers were already working at the furnace, burning bundles of Embassy documents as fast as they could throw them in. The furnace door stood open while they fed papers into the flames, one stack after another. Files, communications, and anything that might have been sensitive were being destroyed as quickly as possible. It was a race against time, and the fire inside that furnace was working as hard as they were.

All around us, there was shouting. Militants were yelling, waving rifles in the air, and making threats toward the Americans inside. Some of them were angry, others looked almost excited, and the noise seemed to echo through the halls and courtyard. It was chaotic and tense, the kind of scene that makes your nerves tighten whether you want them to or not.

But strangely enough, I found myself reacting differently than I might have earlier.

By that point, I had already spent days surrounded by shouting crowds, gunfire, and men waving weapons. Somewhere along the line, it had started to feel almost routine. The constant tension had worn down the edge of fear, replacing it with a kind of numb acceptance.

To be honest, I was getting kind of used to it.

And when I think about that now, it seems pretty sad, doesn't it?

It's hard to believe, but I actually managed to get some sleep that night. After everything that had happened over the past few days, exhaustion finally caught up with me. The floor was not exactly comfortable, but by then, comfort was not something anyone was expecting. Just closing my eyes for a few hours inside the Embassy walls felt like enough.

Chapter 29

Early the next morning, we were up and moving. People gathered their things, what little they had, and boarded the Embassy bus that was supposed to take us to the airport. The idea was simple. Get everyone on the bus, drive to the airport, and get on the evacuation flights.

Freedom was the destination.

Or at least that was the plan.

As the bus pulled out of the Embassy grounds and into the streets of Tehran, it was obvious the city had not settled down overnight. Partygoers were still everywhere. Militants were scattered throughout the streets, many of them still celebrating. Traffic moved slowly, and the bus had to creep forward through crowds of cars and people.

Gunfire echoed around us as we made our way through the city. Pistols and rifles were being fired straight into the air as part of the celebration. To them, it was a victory. To us, it was just another reminder that we were still in the middle of something very unstable.

At one point, a car pulled up beside the bus. One of the passengers inside had a nail gun and was firing it up into the air, laughing as he did it. He was not aiming at the bus or at anyone around him. It was just another part of the celebration for him.

You would think that my biggest concern would have been the militants, the traffic, or the constant sound of gunfire around us.

But oddly enough, that was not what occupied my mind.

All I could think about was where those nails were going to come down.

Every time he fired that nail gun into the air, I found myself watching the sky and wondering where they would land. It seemed like such a small and strange detail compared to everything else happening around us, but that was the thought that stuck in my head.

It is funny how the brain works in moments like that. When you are surrounded by chaos and danger for long enough, your mind sometimes latches onto the smallest and most unexpected things.

We made it to Mehrabad International Airport and unloaded the bus. By the time we stepped off, most of the people on board looked pretty shell-shocked. The ride through the city had taken its toll. Between the crowds, the gunfire, the roadblocks, and the uncertainty of what might happen next, everyone seemed mentally worn down.

It appeared to me that most of the people on the bus were expats who had been living and working in Tehran or Isfahan. Engineers, technicians, office workers, and their families. Many of them had likely spent most of their time going back and forth between their homes and their work sites without really seeing what the streets had become during the revolution.

For a lot of them, that bus ride had probably been their first real look at the militants in full form.

Their general reaction seemed to be pure panic. I could hear people whispering to each other, worried looks on their faces, some talking about how the militants were going to kill us all. The mood felt tense and fearful, like everyone was waiting for something terrible to happen at any moment.

Chapter 30

After what I had been through over the past few days, their hysteria struck me a little differently. I almost found it funny. Not because the situation was safe, but because my perspective had already shifted so much. Compared to the roadblocks, interrogations, burning tires, and the two-day drive across the country, standing at the airport almost felt calm.

From what I had seen, the militants loved making noise and putting on a show. They fired their guns into the air, shouted "death to America," burned American flags, and made all kinds of threats. It was loud, dramatic, and intimidating. But during everything I had experienced on that trip, I had not personally seen them attack or harm anyone directly.

At that moment, my mind was focused on something much simpler.

I was hungry.

After two days of traveling, very little sleep, and almost nothing to eat, food had become my main concern. As we walked into the airport, I started looking around, hoping to see some kind of food vendor or snack stand.

There wasn't one.

And I was still hungry.

Now we had to run the gauntlet through the airport. Militants were everywhere inside the terminal, controlling the flow of people and watching everyone closely. They had set up checkpoints along the way, and nobody was getting past them without being questioned.

They were checking everything. Passports, visas, bags, whatever documents people were carrying. Some of them would open luggage and go through it piece by piece, looking for something that only they seemed to understand. Others stood nearby, asking questions and watching faces as if they were trying to read every reaction.

They wanted to know how much cash we were carrying, where we had come from, and who we worked for. One by one, people stepped forward and answered as best they could while a small group of militants studied papers in their hands.

They had printouts with lists of names on them. Every now and then, one of them would stop someone, point to the paper, and start comparing the spelling of the name in the passport to whatever was written on the sheet. I had no idea where those lists had come from or what they meant.

When my turn came, I handed over my passport and answered their questions as calmly as I could. Inside, I was paying very close attention to everything they were doing. Outside, I tried to look as ordinary and cooperative as possible.

They checked my documents, looked through what little I was carrying, and asked the same questions they were asking everyone else. Where are you from? Where have you been? Who do you work for?

All the while, they kept glancing back at those printouts.

I had no idea what that was all about, and I was smart enough not to ask.

At some point while I was in Yazd, I had decided to cash in all of my travelers' checks at a bank. At the time, it did not seem like an important decision. I simply wanted to have cash on hand instead of carrying the checks around with me.

The teller behind the counter asked a simple question. Did I want the money in U.S. dollars or in another currency? For some reason I still cannot explain, I told him I would take British pounds.

There was no deep thinking behind that choice. No careful planning, no clever strategy. It was just one of those offhand decisions you make without giving it much thought. The teller counted out the pounds, handed them to me, and I went on my way without thinking about it again.

Standing in that airport later, surrounded by militants who were checking passports, asking questions, and wanting to know exactly how much cash everyone was carrying, that little decision suddenly took on a whole new meaning.

If I had been carrying a pocket full of U.S. dollars at that moment, it probably would have attracted a lot more attention than I wanted. Instead, when they checked what money I had, it was British pounds. For whatever reason, that seemed to pass without much interest from them.

Looking back on it now, that small moment at the bank in Yazd feels like one of those strange turns of luck that sometimes show up when you need them most.

This goes back to something I have said before, "There is a God."

The militants, who now controlled the airport, were collecting every greenback they could find. Anyone carrying U.S. dollars was being stopped and questioned about it. If they found cash, they simply took it.

The man standing in front of me had five hundred dollars in his wallet. When they found it, they pulled the bills out, held them up for everyone to see, and then one of them told him, "This is for God." Just like that, his money was gone. There was no argument, no receipt, no discussion.

Standing there watching that exchange made it very clear what was happening. If you were carrying American dollars, they were probably going to end up in someone else's pocket.

I kept my head down and waited for my turn.

Chapter 31

Later on, once we were finally on the airplane and had a little time to breathe again, that same man told me the rest of the story. The five hundred dollars they took was only what he had in his wallet. The real money was hidden somewhere else.

He had thousands of dollars stuffed down inside his cowboy boots.

The militants never thought to check there.

Never underestimate an American cowboy.

When the woman at the checkpoint looked at the money I was carrying and saw British pounds instead of U.S. dollars, she barely gave it a second glance. She waved me through without much interest at all.

Sometimes luck shows up in the smallest ways.

Looking good so far. We boarded the Pan Am, and what a relief that was. After everything it had taken just to reach the airport, stepping onto that airplane felt like crossing an invisible line back toward safety. The seats filled quickly with tired, anxious people who had all been through their own version of the same ordeal.

Then we sat there.

And sat there.

Hours passed without the plane moving. Every now and then, the cabin door would open, and an Iranian official would step on board. They would walk slowly down the aisle, stop beside someone, and ask to see their papers. Passports were checked again, questions asked again, and the tension inside the cabin would rise every time one of them appeared.

No one really spoke much during those visits. People just waited quietly and hoped their documents were in order.

At one point, an American woman was asked to gather her things and step off the plane. The entire cabin went silent as she walked down the aisle and disappeared through the door with the officials. Nobody knew what was happening or why she had been singled out.

A couple of hours later, she came back.

She walked back onto the plane and returned to her seat without much explanation. No announcement was made, and no one seemed to know what had taken place while she was gone. Whatever the issue had been, it must have been resolved because they let her stay.

Still, the waiting continued.

Every minute sitting there felt longer than the last, but at least we were on the airplane. That alone was a step closer to getting out.

Finally, the Boeing 737 doors closed. That simple sound of the cabin door sealing shut carried a sense of relief that is hard to describe. For the first time since stepping onto the plane, it felt like we might actually be leaving.

A few moments later, the engines began to come alive. You could feel the vibration building through the floor and up through the seats as the turbines started to spin. The low hum slowly grew stronger, filling the cabin with that familiar mechanical sound that usually goes unnoticed on ordinary flights.

No one spoke.

The anticipation inside the plane was thick. People sat quietly, some staring straight ahead, others looking out the windows toward the runway. After everything that had happened, I do not think anyone fully believed we were actually about to leave until the wheels lifted off the ground.

For a few minutes, the plane just sat there with the engines running.

Then the Captain's voice came over the intercom. Calm, steady, and professional, the way airline pilots always seem to sound, no matter what is going on outside the cockpit.

He told us he was waiting for taxi instructions and permission to proceed.

And so we waited again.

My father was a flight instructor, and he soloed me when I was sixteen. We flew a 1946 Taylorcraft taildragger, a small, simple airplane that required you to really learn how to fly. There was nothing fancy about it. No complicated systems, no heavy electronics, just an airplane, a set of controls, and the responsibility of handling it correctly.

Back then, flying something like that demanded a good feel for the machine and the air around it. You learned quickly that small airplanes did not forgive sloppy flying. Every takeoff, every landing, every turn required attention and a steady hand.

Chapter 32

Today the old Taylorcraft is not even classified as a full standard aircraft, the way larger planes are. It is generally listed as a sport airplane, just a level or two above what people think of as a powered glider. But at the time, sitting alone in that cockpit at sixteen years old, it felt like the real thing.

With that background, sitting on that Pan Am 737 gave me a different perspective than many of the other passengers. While most people were just focused on getting out of the country, I found myself thinking about what was happening up front in the cockpit.

I knew the routine the pilots were going through.

They were talking with the tower, waiting for clearance, checking their instruments, and going through their procedures step by step. No matter what was happening outside the airplane, airline pilots follow the same disciplined process every time. Engines running, systems checked, communication with ground control, and then eventually clearance to move.

Knowing that helped steady my nerves a little.

It reminded me that up front were professionals who had done this hundreds, maybe thousands of times before. Their job was to fly that airplane safely, and they would not rush anything until they had the instructions they needed.

So while the rest of us sat there wondering if we were really going to leave Iran that day, I could picture exactly what was happening in the cockpit.

They were waiting for the green light.

After a while, the Captain came back on the intercom again. His voice was still calm, but there was a slight edge to it this time. He told us that we were going to taxi out toward the runway. Then he added something that immediately tightened the air inside the cabin.

He said he was getting no response from the control tower.

That was not good.

For an airliner, communication with the tower is part of the normal routine before any movement on the runway. Taxi clearance, takeoff clearance, all of it usually comes through that line of communication. Without it, things become uncertain very quickly.

Still, the plane slowly began to move.

We could feel the gentle motion as the aircraft rolled away from the gate and started taxiing across the airport. Outside the windows, the runway lights and airport buildings passed by slowly, while inside the cabin, everyone remained quiet. The tension that had been building all morning seemed to grow heavier with every minute.

I kept thinking about what the pilots must have been discussing up front. With no response from the tower, they were probably trying every frequency they had available, hoping someone would answer. At the same time, they had to decide what to do if no one ever responded.

Back then, I had enough flying experience to understand that this was not a normal situation. Airplanes do not just take off from major international airports without talking to the tower first.

Which meant the men in the cockpit were now facing a decision.

And whatever that decision was going to be, we were all along for the ride.

This was totally against all international aviation regulations. The control tower normally runs everything at an airport. Nothing moves without their permission and instructions. Aircraft wait their turn, follow taxi directions, and only enter the runway when the tower clears them to do so.

The standard procedure is simple and disciplined. When a plane reaches the runway, it pauses for a final check. The pilots review their instruments, confirm the flight plan, and wait for the tower to issue instructions. The tower provides the departure heading, the altitude to climb to, and the clearance to move onto the runway.

None of that happened.

From my seat, I could feel the airplane continue taxiing without stopping. A moment later, I felt the turn as we rolled off the taxiway and onto the runway itself. There had been no clearance, no radio call, no instructions from the tower.

Permission was not asked for, and it clearly was not needed anymore.

The plane never slowed down. As we turned onto the runway, the engines surged harder, the sound rising quickly inside the cabin. The pilot pushed the throttles forward even before we were perfectly lined up with the centerline. The aircraft straightened itself as it accelerated, gathering speed faster and faster.

Everyone on board could feel what was happening.

That pilot had made his decision.

Chapter 33

Looking back on it now, I have a lot of respect for the man sitting in that cockpit. He understood the situation better than anyone else on that airplane. Waiting around for formal clearance in the middle of a revolution was not going to get us anywhere.

He did what needed to be done.

I liked that pilot.

He wanted to get us home.

The plane lifted off and no one said a word. For a few moments, the cabin stayed completely quiet. People sat there holding their breath, almost afraid to celebrate too early. After everything that had happened, no one wanted to believe we were really out until we were well clear of the country.

A short time later, the Captain's voice came over the intercom.

"This is the Captain. We are now leaving Iranian airspace."

That was the moment everything changed.

The silence inside the plane exploded into a roar. People started laughing, clapping, shouting. Some passengers hugged each other while others simply leaned back in their seats with the kind of relief that only comes after days of fear and uncertainty. It felt like the entire plane had been holding its breath, and now everyone could finally let it out.

The skeleton crew working the flight quickly brought out the drink carts. It was not exactly standard service, but under the circumstances, nobody was worried about the rules. The drinks were on the house, and people gladly accepted them.

The cabin turned into a celebration.

Songs began breaking out here and there as the tension drained away. A few people tried different tunes, but the one that seemed to spread the most was the same one over and over.

"Take Me Home, Country Roads, West Virginia…"

Before long, much of the cabin was singing along. It was not exactly a polished choir, but nobody cared. The words carried a kind of meaning at that moment that went far beyond the music.

After the chaos, the roadblocks, the interrogations, and the long journey across the country, we were finally heading away from it all.

The pilot pointed the aircraft west, and we made a straight line for Paris.

I thought about it for a moment.

I'm going to Paris.

Hummmm.

That idea rolled around in my head while the plane continued west. I had been in the desert longer than was probably good for me. For months, my world had been dry mountains, dusty roads, and long stretches of land where the most common sights were sheep, goats, and the occasional camel wandering across the horizon.

Life had become very simple out there. Work, heat, dust, and the same rugged scenery day after day.

Now suddenly I was headed to Paris.

Chapter 34

The contrast between the two places could not have been greater. One moment you are crossing deserts and dealing with roadblocks in the middle of a revolution, and the next you are flying toward one of the most famous cities in the world.

It did not take long for me to make up my mind.

I decided I needed to lay over in Paris for a day or two. After everything that had happened, it seemed like a perfectly reasonable idea. A little time in a city filled with lights, restaurants, and people enjoying normal life sounded pretty appealing.

Besides, after weeks of desert landscapes, I figured it might be good for my sanity to see something other than sheep, goats, and camels for a while.

The Grumman company had a large number of people on the plane leaving Tehran. In those final weeks of the revolution, thousands of American civilians, engineers, and contractors were being evacuated from Iran as the situation collapsed around them.

When we landed in Paris, buses and taxis were already waiting for the Grumman group. They were organized, had people on the ground, and knew exactly where their employees were supposed to go. Watching that operation unfold made things feel a lot more normal again after the chaos we had just left behind.

I felt very comfortable being around that group. After days of roadblocks, interrogations, and militants waving rifles, simply being among Americans again was reassuring. I looked the part well enough and acted as if I belonged there, so when the Grumman people started heading toward their transportation, I just loaded up with them.

No one questioned it.

At customs, the officials seemed to recognize the group right away. The Grumman employees were waved straight through the airport without much trouble at all. They moved through together, collected their things, and headed toward the taxis waiting outside to take them to the hotels.

And me?

I went right along with them.

I smiled as a good Grumman employee should.

I had a nice single room, paid for by Grumman. After everything that had happened over the previous few days, simply being inside a quiet hotel room felt like stepping into another world. No shouting crowds, no gunfire in the distance, no checkpoints or roadblocks to worry about.

The first thing I did was call down to the front desk and ask if the hotel had a laundry service. They told me they did. I asked them to send someone up to collect my clothes. I had been wearing the same things for far longer than anyone should, and by that point, they had been through deserts, roadblocks, airports, and a long flight out of the country.

Before long, someone came to the door to pick them up.

With that taken care of, I stepped into the shower and let the hot water run. It was probably the longest and most relaxing shower I had taken in a very long time. The tension from the past few days slowly began to fade as the water washed away the dust and fatigue from the trip.

Afterward, wrapped in a hotel robe, I finally lay down on the bed.

Real sleep came easily.

When morning arrived, my clothes were already waiting for me. Cleaned, pressed, and neatly folded, as if nothing unusual had ever happened to them at all. It was a small detail, but after everything I had just been through, it felt like a luxury.

I had lunch in the hotel restaurant. It was the first real meal I had been able to sit down and enjoy in quite a while. The pace was calm, the room was quiet, and the atmosphere felt worlds away from the chaos I had just left behind. For the first time in days, I could simply relax and eat without worrying about roadblocks, militants, or what might happen next.

While I was there, I ended up talking with the bartender. He asked where I had come from, and before long, I was explaining where I had been and what the past few days had been like. I told him about the trip across the desert, the checkpoints, the airport, and finally the flight out.

When I finished, he just nodded.

He understood.

Then he smiled in a way that suggested he had already decided what I needed next. Without making a big production out of it, he picked up the phone and called a cab for me. When the driver arrived, the bartender stepped outside and spoke with him in French for a moment.

I had no idea what he said, but it seemed to cover everything that needed saying.

The driver nodded, I climbed into the back seat, and we headed into town.

It was time for a little catching up in Paris.

Chapter 35

After a few days in Paris, I decided it was time to head back to the States. The short break had done me some good, but home was starting to sound better and better. I went back to the airport and had my ticket reissued for a flight to JFK.

With that taken care of, I found a seat near the gate and waited for my flight number to appear on the departure board. It felt strange sitting there in a calm, orderly airport after everything that had happened over the previous week. People moved about casually, travelers read newspapers, and announcements came over the loudspeaker in that steady airport rhythm.

Then suddenly I heard gunshots.

They sounded very close. Sharp cracks that echoed through the terminal.

I was used to hearing gunfire by then, but not that close and not inside an airport. My reaction was immediate. I hit the deck.

I stayed there for a moment before slowly opening my eyes.

I was the only one on the floor.

Everyone else was still sitting in their chairs, walking around, or continuing their conversations like absolutely nothing had happened. No one looked alarmed, no one was diving for cover, and no one seemed to notice anything unusual.

That was when I realized I might have overreacted just a little.

I got up, brushed myself off, and quietly reseated myself, trying to look as normal as possible. I glanced around a few times and then asked a couple of people nearby what had just happened.

It turned out the airport was installing new automatic doors.

Workers were using jackhammers to break up some concrete for the installation. The sound had echoed through the terminal in a way that made it resemble gunshots.

After everything I had just experienced, my brain had gone straight to the worst possible conclusion.

It took a moment, but I finally leaned back in my chair and let out a small laugh.

Apparently, I had spent just a little too long around real gunfire.

I never saw Fanar or the man behind the desk again. One day, they were simply gone. In a place where people disappeared quickly and quietly during those months, that was not entirely surprising, but it still left questions that were never answered.

After I got back home and finally settled in, things were not completely normal right away. For about two years, I had nightmares off and on. They were not constant, but every now and then, something would bring it all back. The roadblocks, the shouting crowds, the gunfire in the streets, and the long drive across the desert would replay in my sleep. It takes time for the mind to sort through experiences like that.

Life eventually moved forward, as it always does.

Then, later that same year, the situation in Iran took another dramatic turn. On November 4, 1979, militants made the final assault on the American Embassy in Tehran. Ninety people were taken hostage during the takeover, and fifty-two Americans were held captive for 444 days. The crisis lasted until January 20, 1981, when they were finally released.

Watching that unfold from back home gave me a strange perspective. I could not help thinking about the night I had spent inside that same Embassy compound, only months before everything changed again.

People sometimes ask if I would do it all again.

The honest answer is probably.

Experiences like that change you. They are difficult, unpredictable, and sometimes frightening, but they also become part of the story of your life. Looking back, I would not say it was easy, but it was certainly something I will never forget.

-Grady Lee Honeycutt